'Unless I understand the conquests of Alexander as a dying soldier's pain and thirst, unless I grasp the ideas of the Inquisition as the torn body of the heretic, unless I feel that these sufferings are my own, unless in other words I have charity, my ideas of evil are empty.'

Jeffrey Burton Russell, *The Devil: Perceptions of Evil from Antiquity to Primitive Christianity.*

The Night
the Dog Smiled

John Newlove

ECW PRESS

CANADIAN CATALOGUING IN PUBLICATION DATA

Newlove, John, 1938-
  The night the dog smiled

Poems.
ISBN 0-920763-33-2 (bound) – ISBN 0-920763-31-6 (pbk.)

I. Title.

PS8527.E94N53 1986   C811'.54   C86-093270-2
PR9199.3.N4N53 1986

Published by ECW PRESS, 307 Coxwell Avenue, Toronto,
Ontario M4L 3B5 with the assistance of The Canada
Council and the Ontario Arts Council.

Some of these poems have previously appeared in *The
Canadian Forum, Canadian Literature, The Capilano
Review, The Contemporary Canadian Poem Anthology*
(Coach House Press), *Contemporary Verse 2, Descant,
Event, Freelance, From a Window, Gnosis,* Gorse Press
(broadsheets), *Grain, The Greenfield Review, The Green
Plain* (Oolichan Books), The Hamilton Poetry Centre
(broadsheet), *The Headless Angel, Island, Island*
broadsheet, *Jewish Dialogue, The Malahat Review,
Quarry, The Riverside Quarterly, Sailing the Road
Clear, Saturday Night, Writing,* and *Zest.*

The Canada Council kindly gave me financial assistance. The Head of the Thomas Fisher Rare Book Library, Richard Landon, and the Manuscript Librarian there, Rachel Grover, were of great help to me in locating old notes and drafts, one of which is used here. And I owe the title of 'The Permanent Tourist Comes Home' to a phrase of P.K. Page's.

CONTENTS

to the Whitton-Milroys

DRIVING

You never say anything in your letters. You say,
I drove all night long through the snow
in someone else's car
and the heater wouldn't work and I nearly froze.
But I know that. I live in this country too.
I know how beautiful it is at night
with the white snow banked in the moonlight.

Around black trees and tangled bushes,
how lonely and lovely that driving is,
how deadly. You become the country.
You are by yourself in that channel of snow
and pines and pines,
whether the pines and snow flow backwards smoothly,
whether you drive or you stop or you walk or you sit.

This land waits. It watches. How beautifully desolate
our country is, out of the snug cities,
and how it fits a human. You say you drove.
It doesn't matter to me.
All I can see is the silent cold car gliding,
walled in, your face smooth, your mind empty,
cold foot on the pedal, cold hands on the wheel.

In summer we were disappointed
with the open. We had stood
the winter, hoping for stronger winds
to prove our worth;
this was a foolish pride,
as good as any other.

But in the summer we were discontented
with the easiness, not being accustomed
to freedom, and it was
the cities we longed for,
the fabulous, the anonymous,
not the summer but the rush.

It was the cities we entered
instead of entering manhood;
and we never saw a thing, I least of all,
until one day my eyes opened briefly.

Then it was disgust I saw,
it was fear of ourselves I saw,
so that we ceased to live and only moved,
and my eyes closed
and I wrote sweet lyrics,
la la la la la....

Then I was angry, foolishly,
for not having seen, I wanted to cry:
Burn your delicious cars,
Crush down the electric towers,
Throw out the mechanisms
that work so well
until they die, no love
until they die.

It was too late. My eyes
were closed. Freedom, summer,
never seemed to be what we wanted.

A CRESCENT

A crescent stretches shining back
to the past. The last of the triumphs
is resplendent, is unified, is prosperous,
falls in disorder and riot.

The tenants of the land are like a storm,
the old melodies consist of one song,
the spirits will even whistle,
the river is blood.

But despair is not a policy.
Populations learn to carry burdens,
they build an armoured cathedral: next
to nothing.

The earth has been created
many times, in the minds of men
the centre, the axis, the pivot of the universe.
The crescent rises and shines.

A ROOM

A room of charming, beautiful, ineffectual men,
drunk, surrounded by painted chairs
in green and gold, black plumes carved into them,
stacked, dust sheets everywhere: and women
losing their patience over the centuries
with this wasteful, foolish elegance,
all this nonsense that made knives
the best sculpture, and missiles. There is a silence
in this room, of waiting for the end,
of killers waiting for their victims' permissions
before those knives descend.

1.

To the oppressed
nothing is left but song,
which the rich will adopt in a more melodious form.
Even your voice will be stolen from you
and the rhythm of your chains will be modulated
by choirs of celestial beings – which is necessary:
okay, okay, obey,
since your only function is to die.

2.

Speak.
Speak. But be careful of making moulds
which the spiritually illiterate
can fill up with gumbo.

3.

Guarded and guided,
the fact before hypothesis: early morning,
somewhere in the time
that I was, this simple apparition –
my small mother, orange flannel nightgown,
early light. Wee Willie Winkie, her finger
to her lips, walks in slow motion
on her delicate ankles,
sibilant, saying Shh, shh,
Father's dead.

4.

I wake up
and sit on the edge of the bed.
You sparrow, mother, you beautiful sparrow.

5.

I love you. Father is not dead.
Time is dead. There is a scoop in time
whatever self my self is
returns to every time, my grey sweet mother.

6.

Well, to die in the Spring
and be buried in the muck
seems reasonable. Enough
of this. The mountains are bright tonight
outside my window, and passing by.
Awkwardly, I am in love again.

The ground that looks so firm is bog,
that ground is death, corpses lurk in it,
dead houses. The city is quiet, not thinking,
where
is everyone? Today?

The forest had seemed full of people in their various skins,
it was as if the malevolent bears
could at least be reasoned with, the deer
able to discuss their fears, defending
a dangerous way of life. When we think cold we feel cold.
It is the same, they would say.
When we feel cold we think cold.

But where is everyone?
Isn't there anything but cigarettes in this city,
red marks in the night, isn't there anything
besides the cars that crawl
along their crowded routes, tunnels,
and painful buildings, is there nothing
but me after all? Did I dream this,
this world – all there is?

I had thought of rocks,
of green, I had thought
of shells, I was the one who had considered wood,
seas, animals flexing,
that was it: I had thought of humans,
pitiful and pleasing in their disease of life,
disease of time, disease of strife;
but there was no one here but me at all,
on this ground.

Make it easier, they say, make it easier. Tell
me something I already know, about stars or flowers or,
or happiness. I am happy sometimes, though
not right now, specially. Things are not going
too good right now. But you should try
to cheer people up, they say. There is
a good side to life, though
not right now, specially. Though the stars
continue to shine in some places and the flowers
continue to bloom in some places
and people do not starve in some places
and people are not killed in some places
and there are no wars in some places
and there are no slaves in some places
and in some places people love each other,
they say. Though I don't know where. They say,
I don't *want* to be sad. Help me not to know.

from YUKICHI FUKUZAWA

I turned away astonished with my own face
full of tears and beer on my breath. My
enemies smiled to each other and decided
to be kind.
        Why does this fool love?
I sit sad   quiet   like a priest
doing penance. I was bold
when I was young.
I should hide from my brothers.

O
bigoted saints
who fear to act and distress others
there are no police for your souls.
You will live to eat the adulation
of those who put up with you
because of your age.

The golden fish curl around the trees
the branches   waiting. Be
a happy child.

You know people wait for you to die.
I will take bitter medicine.
This hardship is pleasure.

Small human figures and fanciful monsters
abound. Dreams surround us,
preserve us. We praise constancy as brave,
but variation's lovelier.

Rain surrounds us, arguments and dreams, there are
forests between us, there are
too many of us for comfort, always were.

                             Is civilization
only a lack of room, only
an ant-heap at last? – the strutting cities
of the East, battered gold,
the crammed walls of India,
humanity swarming, indistinguishable
                          from the earth?

Even the nomads roaming the green plain, for them
at last no land was ever enough.

Spreading – but now we can go anywhere
                         and we are afraid
and talk of small farms instead of the stars
                       and all the places we go
space is distorted.

How shall we save the symmetry of the universe? —
or our own symmetry, which is the same.

                                   Which myths
should capture us, since we do not wish
to be opened, to be complete? —
or are they all the same, all of them?

Now a dream involves me, of a giant sprawled among stars,
face to the dark, his eyes closed.
                                   Common.

Only he is not breathing, he does not heave.
Is it Gulliver? — huge, image of us, tied, webbed in,
and never learning anything,

                                   always ignorant,
always amazed, always capable of delight,
and giving it, though ending in hatred, but
an image only. Of disaster. But there is no disaster.
It is just that we lose joy and die.

But is there a symmetry?
                                    Is there reason
in the galaxies – Or is this all glass,
a block bubbled in a fire, accident only,
prettiness fused without care, pettiness,
though some logic, alien but understandable,
in the ruined crystal?

                                    The forests, the forests, swaying
there is no reason why they should be beautiful.
They live for their own reasons, not ours.
But they are.

It is not time that flows but the world.

And the world flows
still flows. Even in these worn-out days,
worn-out terms,
once in a while our poets
must
speak

of Spring! Of all things! The flowers
blow in their faces too, and they smell perfumes,
and they are seduced
by colour – rural as the hairy crocus or urban as a waxy tulip.

But confusion. The world
flows past. It is hard to remember age. Does
this always world flow? Does it? Please say it does,
not time.
Do not say time flows.
Say: We do. Say: We live.

Fly-speck, fly-speck. In this ever island Earth
we are the tiny giants, swaggering
behind the dinosaurs, lovely,
tame brontosaurus, sweet cows lumbering
among the coal trees, fronds offering
shade and future fuel.

And the land around us green and happy,
waiting as you wait for a killer to spring,
a full-sized blur,
waiting like a tree in southern Saskatchewan,
remarked on, lonely and famous as a saint.

The mechanisms by which the stars generate invention
live all over and around us
and yet we refine machines, defer
to tricks as discovery. Everything is always here,
and burning.

There are no surprises, there is only
what is left. We live
inside the stars,

                                burning, burning,
the mechanisms.

Stars, rain, forests.
Stars rain forests.
Sew up the lives together. There is
this only world. Thank God: this World
and its wrapped variations
spreading around and happy, flowing,
flowing through the climate of intelligence,
beautiful confusion looking around,
seeing the mechanics and the clouds
and marvelling, O Memory …

ONE THING

1.

In the waterfalls
the dance of sound

In the air
the dance of light

Or reversed, no matter

2.

Rowers dancing
heel & toe
in circe's hell

The death dance
of various legions
across the rhine

Medieval angels

Bombs
in asia

3.

In the waterfalls
the dance of light &
the dance of sound

In the air
all one thing

4.

In the forests
heavy animals move
on fire
among the trees.

A low, empty-
looking, unpainted house;
back of it, the corn
blighted, the tractor
abandoned.

The enemy cats are sneaking through the back.
That's why she sits on the bathroom windowsill
with her tail waving.

All night long. And it's a long jump down tile
onto the porcelain bathtub bottom,
then hurdling the side to the floor.

When I get up she comes out, rubbing her flea-y cheeks
in repetition against me, against my leg.
So I feed her. She's tired.
And the enemy cats are sneaking up.

DRIED-OUT INSECTS

The turtles in the Sorestad's bathroom
have beautiful markings
but look vicious.

I sit here shitting
and they sit there sitting
and acting mean.

I'm just trying to be clean,
but afraid to move. Can turtles fly?
I know they can't.
But they might try.

Meanwhile, like wives,
they waver in the water,
beautiful and vicious.

NOTE TO ROSENBLATT

This plant has such a protocol about it
that we must watch the feeding
more than the flowering. How can its food
seem to be only water and the moderate sun?
Where does colour come from? –
jumping out of the broken husk,
a punch in the guts of pessimists!

VISITING THE PURDYS, 1973

Eurithe is rearranging the trees
with cutters
like a maniac hydro lineman
up on the mantlepiece
of his own home
ordering the knickknacks.

It sounds like a giant cracking his knuckles
off in the bush, concealed and shy.

Al puts a cardboard box of crumpled paper
out in the driveway, some sort
of special place of its own – no,
now he's set fire to it,
trying to burn the forest down, I guess.

And the flames rise,
diluted in the sun.

Al walks over to watch a tree.
I think she has the delusion
she's sawing the sky down, he says to me.

I'm sawing down the blocks
to the sky, Eurithe says.

Why don't you saw down the whole damned tree?

I've thought of that, says she.

He is the nervous hunter.
Words, women, whisky, even wisdom,
are his game; he admits
to no favourite order.

He follows any road,
looking at everything.
No tree escapes his inspection,
and horses are not safe either.

This week his baldness
assaults the radio; next,
his wine rusts an island, a junta
feels the weight of his cigar.

Back and forth he wanders,
asking questions. He ought to have
a greasy grey felt hat
pushed back on his head. Perhaps he has.

I can see those shoes of his
plumb in the middle of a forest;
that hand grabbing a beer
at the north pole; that wet cigar
shining, just like a bloody star.

LIKE WATER

I wish my love could
be taken for granted.

It's just there like water,
always present, unfrozen.

This is not to be a desert
we inhabit.

Well, it's full of your poems, my life,
those oases I never thought I'd need,
and resentments towards your enemies,
as if I hadn't made enough of my own.
A couple of nights ago a friend visited me,
he's a good young poet, though
I don't know what young means any more, dammit,
I miss you, oasis: that I thought I
would never need.

Svejk said, 'marjoram
smells like an ink-bottle
    in a valley of flowering acacias.
On the hill....'
            A clerk interrupted
imploringly, the smell
(my dear the smell was dreadful) floated
in the wooden office.
            God,
the furniture was beautiful.
               If

only
there
were
woman
in it, in the bottle, in the breeze.

TORONTO NOVEMBER

As the first inevitable snow falls
the drivers pretend
they have never seen such a thing
before. I cannot
blame them. I cannot stand it.
On the radio this morning
they said that a garbage truck
had fallen over onto a car. I would have liked
to have seen it. Now the garbage
is falling out of the sky. And *when*
will those skinny high-priced models in magazines
stop pretending in full colour
that we like this stuff, that we are like
this stuff? God: give me some warmth for once
and I will then do you the favour
of belief. You cannot exist without me.
How easy religion must be
on sunny islands, in regions where nothing freezes....

All day long
    in my factory
I sing the same song,
    grumbling, refractory,

twisting my reasons
    for hating the place,
in all seasons
    noting the change by the space

given in orders to eggs
    or to peppermint canes,
ducking among the legs
    and tables, sprains

in my fingers and thumbs;
    looking for reason, to grab it,
and complaining of slums
    I force myself to inhabit.

COLD, HEAT

Life gets more extreme as it goes on.
I don't remember these temperatures
going up and down so much
when I was younger. God:
am I going to die?

Then, the heat was only heat,
the cold, cold. Now
every bone aches with questions.

BIG MIRROR

I am in dentist's chair leaning back.

You are evil dentist banging on tools.
Opening and shutting drawers in cabinets.

You're toothchipper sliding around behind me.

You conferring behind hand.
Whispering to nurse about me.

You hate my teeth.

I know her too.

But you the one hustling in and out of room.
Killing time jingling instruments.
Rattling sheets x-ray film adjusting lights.
Waiting for me to be afraid so you can begin.

What use hurting me if not afraid?
Job must have other compensation than monetary.

I know you fat face no hair on head.
Soft red bulging lips estimating me.

I know you blotched purple and white skin face.
I know trembly hand waiting with excitement
to rape mouth of me.

I know what needles and chrome in there
you want to stick.

I am I said in dentist's chair leaning back.

There on ceiling stand upside-down
black transparent flies immobilized in horror
at what you going to do to me.

You never pulled fly's tooth.
You never pulled fly's tooth.

Black flies never knowing what like
to have long tooth roots drawn slow out of jaw.
Feel hard part of body suctioned out of body.

Long pull not know.

But feel sorry for me sitting in dentist's chair.
Horrified you bald man dentist.

Short white coat dentist in background always.

Head of me bolted so can't turn or discover
secret dirty work only mind knows.

Start soon now getting scared.

What you will do to me with help smiling blonde.
Nurse receptionist bleach maybe too much.
Greasy lipstick red on big mouth grinning.
Hate men except fat dentist sometimes who hurts.
Pays money to buy javex lipstick.

Sorry of flies no good.

Ridiculous caught in dentist's chair looking at ceiling.
Painted green reflects light.

Big mirror on cabinet in corner can see from corner of eye
self and look dumb tied rigor-mortis here
and gagged cotton snick machine
takes inside wrong picture on other side of room.

Snick estimates me.

I am safe look like pay insurance.
Or work and will grunt hurt and screw up eyes good.

Evil damn dentist comes fast around
left side of chair holding weapons.

Now start fat man

SHAKESPEARE'S SONNETS

for Paul Dutton

I'm not interested in rainbows
but in the sky itself, the serene
not the spectacular: the permanent.

This is a business of trying to make things permanent,
not ephemeral. What else to do?
We know we die, so chase notoriety too.

All the couples of Shakespeare's sonnets
make sense to me. It was another love
other than the Dark One he reached for.

Us.

He was a very old man. I felt old myself. We were
having dinner together. He had ordered. It seemed like a
kind of courtesy on my part but, in fact, I was shy of my
ignorance.

He said, Aren't you going to interview me?

I said that I had been sent to do that but I couldn't think
of anything to say.

He looked at me out of the coroner of his eye. He said,
Good.

We had lemon sole and some sort of white wine I liked. I
wished we could have had a bottle each, rather than
sharing one between us.

Even after the wine I couldn't think of anything to ask.
Him. I thought, Dammit, I'm just a Canadian. Ah,
Goddam paranoia.

Pretty enjoyable, though. Good stuff.

Again he said, Aren't you going to interview me?

My mouth was full of fish.

After I swallowed, I thought of the next best thing. I
said, No. But I'll tell you what I'll do. I'll get invited to
parties for years because of this.

He said, Up yours. There's about a half glass of wine each. Shall we share it?

I said, No. I want it all. If you want any more order another bottle. You're bloody rich. I don't mind you being rich but I resent your being a good writer.

He said, That's what you all say. I'm an old man. A very old man. I'm going to bed. Waiter.

He walked off. The waiter came with another bottle of wine and the bill.

That's what you get for being famous, I thought. Your kidneys can't take it any more. I'd like to be able to treat people like that. Jesus, I want to be famous, I thought.

The world's longest poem didn't start like this
didn't go on like this
it doesn't end like this – there was still
a cigarette burning. After
the ending, after all the Indians
the Pygmies, the Gypsies, the Jews
the burned and the black and the spurned
after all the cheated and demeaned were buried by bulldozers
or sold as cheap souvenirs in green translucent glass
that cigarette still fumed –
what wealth!

And the writer of all that stuff
was still stupid
he still thought that when people said
I understand
they understood

He didn't know that he lied for pleasure
others, profit
and he still saw
all-around wrap-around death and didn't believe it
and woke up one night in the maw and believed it

Knowing what was wanted

Not these sweaty visions everyone has
no recognizable rhythms
no beauty in the line
no knowledge
                    only noise
no feeling of pain

This whole civilization is noise
we are not wholly beasts yet
but the politicians roar at us
until civilization is minor

And we are surrounded by liars
so that when the poet that is in us says
we are surrounded by liars
he is called a liar
or is given prizes, liar
obligations

O I am sick and called sick
and I am healthier than you are

At least I know how lovely we are

Enduring –

Which is history
we are one after the other
we are the stars of this show
but we are
at the end of all time

What nonsense we talk
What nonsense we're told
What nonsense we are

But I wanted to tell you still how lovely we are
of the ages of jewels
of failed cities
of the notion that there was good
how this century began like all the others

in blood
and milk-white dreams
and ended
with insect hopes
with insect hopes
all in a heap
like all the others
who ever died

SYLLABLES

via Sanskrit

1.

A stranger sings in the village at night:
listening to the heavy sound of clouds:
black in a sullen sky: tears in his eyes:
he sings a song of his loneliness: his longing.

The listeners to those nearby sounds know
how like death distance from a lover is:
how like death: even pride is forgotten:
they too even refuse to say goodbye to it.

2.

Black smoke from a dirty fire:
these clouds: covering the whole
sky: and the fresh thick grass is
a dark mat on the earth: it
is the time for love: when those
who are alone must sing their
songs softly: only to death.

3.

Alone in her husband's house she hears
from far away the slow warm spring
vibrating sound of black bees
moving among the birds –
tremulous music
of love. She hears
shyly, so
shyly
longs
:

4.

Through tears she saw the lovely
masses of clouds
grouping in a dark sky: 'Love,
if you leave me
now ...' she said: holding me: her
legs moving: words
turn away helplessly from
what she did then.

5.

Like a shy woman showing:
for the first time: in love: her thighs:
the sandy beds of autumn rivers.

IN THE FOREST

They are called children
of the forest but
know themselves

by a different name

the translation of which
I cannot give you.

There is a villager and there is
forestman, pygmy –

the villager despising
the forestman for his shortness

(the legs disproportionate
to the body)

while the forestman knows
the villager's noisy
clumsy
ways in the green bush.

Nothing is strange.

Each thinks to have
an advantage

of the other, each
thinks he has –

the villagers eager
to bring the pygmies
within the power
of their spirit-world –

pygmies co-operating
knowing that rituals call
for feasts, the funeral feast,
for example.

Their own custom prescribes
a quick and unceremonious
disposal of the dead.

But rituals mean
food, hospitality.

They submit
as far as possible.

After, the boys
who have gone   (such trouble)
in a well-fed rite
to become adults in the village

return home
to the forest clearings.

They sit on the laps of their mothers
to show their knowledge:

they are still children
in the real world
surrounded by villages,

in the forest.

Coda

Villagers, what will you do?

Will you have forestmen succumbing
to sun on the new plantations?

They say: When the forest dies
we die, they
who love the shaded forest,

you who fear the shadowed forest
where the long ominous
bush-slashing heavy-bladed
knife is used.

SPEECH ABOUT A BLACKFOOT WOMAN
WITH TRAVOIS, PHOTO BY R.H. TRUEMAN

ca. 1890

Yes, yes, they never developed the wheel.
Or the gun. Cheap sarcasm. Here is the queen
of the prairie, holding a sad white horse
not by the rein (a string, really) in her hand
but by being there. She is taller than the horse
and darker. Even in her foreign clothes
there is regality. Time for a metaphor. She stares.
The land stretches. That's not a metaphor,
that is the truth. The horizon looks like a line
drawn by Brian Fisher, exact and ambiguous.
She's dead now. I love her. I guess.
Don't like the horse much. It's dead too.

I want to be good.
I should
stop.
*

Having done what I could,
should I have done
what I should?
*

The pygmies laugh in the forest
after they eat the Bantu's meat.

When they cry
they sit on the laps
of their mothers.
*

Crying children,
we are too small.
*

Will you forgive me
my attempts to forgive you?
*

Can this last longer?
Can this longing last?
*

Yes. Yes.

THE LIGHT OF HISTORY: THIS RHETORIC AGAINST THAT JARGON

When the day comes that these cries will be ridiculous mementoes,
some amusing fable, ununderstandable
even in the light of history, then God bless you happy people.
It would be my wish that you could not comprehend
sadness or cruelty, but lived your vigorous lives in peace.

There is time enough, has been, for understanding.
To Hell with it. So long as the green Earth grows
and the great stars shine, live on and love each other.
Being is admirable and the graceful trees in the wind
sway in concert with you in this ever deathless world.

1.

I walked like a cat behind my father.

2.

This turbulent ear hears turbulent music,
the poem made up of its parts.

3.

I have a picture of her,
smiling

She was smiling at the camera,
not me

       She would be in silks
       She would be wary & rough
       under the sheets   (under the stuff)

The boldness of her innocence

       You wouldn't care

       What do you remember
       after you've been happy?

4.

The message is that there is no message.
You can't live forever on resentment.

The thing is whether to stuff stuff
into the middle or into
the many endings.

I have a picture,
of you smiling

Single-minded pervert.

My lips are sour and the voice won't speak.

She put on a garment of gaiety and courage
the night the Dog smiled

I myself
am impatient with myself

I know you don't lie to me
Your lies are aimed only at yourself,
the only one you must and can
not convince. Never believing, you.

INSTRUCTIONS FOR PATIENTS

Watch out for sharp pieces of bone.

A poor frail body

She wants to know why her parents
seem like leftovers
from last year

By subdividing ages
of evolutionary stages

We live in an eternal Now
the estuaries of an ancient sea
the past of saints
and devils & miracles

It is insane to pretend to be insane.

You cannot reveal yourself.
You cannot conceal yourself.

It is necessary only to be relentless

Stamping your feet like horses——

5.

Look, you always gave me
good things, you. Yourself. That you sent me,
trustingly. That I wear like a beautiful
bright silk badge. That I didn't earn, but that
I wear for bravery.

I liked it because I had no other choice,
a dancer out of time.

In the forest
heavy animals move

water, a black trickle of spilt ink
among the blazing rocks——

——habits of description.

No, not yours, you'll say,
and you know you lie
but you have to say.

I wish I were lying with you now. Lovely.
But tried and tired. Taught. And in tears.
Indeed. Freezing.

6.

This is about ridges of bone, this
is about the evil your desire does, this
is in the night the Dog smiles,
this is about you.

It is necessary to be relentless.
That can't be the end of it,
still treading the prison corridors
of the empty mountains
                                    Looking
at her and thinking

The train was standing in the station
waiting exactly where I had left it
months earlier,
                            looking older

Stamping its feet like horses.

Look, what
was once done with passion is now done with love,
and more slowly

The solid rock becomes an open door
in a huge explosion of night

The words slid sideways. Wise.

I kept looking out the window to see
if it was Spring yet,
but Winter was still on the mountains,
looking in the window
to see if I'd grown young yet or if
my hair was dark again

How can I grow up if I was never young?

And then he saw
that he was secure
in his cultivation
of this minute garden.

Oh.

& your belief can't make it true, your
doubt won't make it false

O my largest milieu is belief

Not the end of nature

of living out this life of evil, of desire, of acting

You cannot reveal yourself
You prefer the blood of death
to the blood of birth

   She put on a garment

You cannot conceal yourself

   She would be

in silks.

The message is that there is no message.

We are part of the tomb itself,
not of the furnishings.

This death is not the end of nature,
but of fault——

    These insulted empires
    These Cambodias
    These Ethiopias

——the expression of sadness on their faces
as they killed

This night the Dog smiled,
strange, brave, and unlucky Comrade

remembering pain almost with affection.

7.

The train was standing in
the station, waiting exactly where
it had left us years
earlier, looking older,
stamping its feet

She wants to know why her lovers
look like leftovers

The boldness of her

      Look, nobody gets wise writing
      Now I must be making
      pretty manners
      at you
      It's necessary to realize that all these phrases
      are stolen. The arrangement is all.

You about to turn away,
this is what I almost wanted to say

      The web traps you, not
      others
              ——the wounded hills.

His voice coloured. He
felt
    something
    about Hafez
    something about the Chinese
    something
romantic.

It's lonely here and I'm going mad.

I'd rather be a toy to you than
nothing at all to you.
I'm not talking to you.

> Something he would like to have.
> Something she would like to be.

Emotional forgers.

'——beautiful women were moved
to the strongest emotion'

> *The Tireless Traveller.*

the tireless traveller says
you never say anything in your letters.

> Blue lakes and the mountains
get thirsty too. All the day long.

A low, empty-
looking, unpainted house.
Back of it, the corn
blighted, the tractor
abandoned.

This earth is a body.

He feels
like a giant wrinkled spider spinning his web
for himself
and it is not like sitting on a bus dreaming
of women, she
turned suddenly and kissed him on the mouth
violently and he didn't know what to do in
his shame———

      Anxious and asking.
      He did not know where her eyes were.
      He did not know where his eyes were.

Constantly thinking.
You. In silks.

8.

      In the edge
      of a painful century

Some things are more important than the truth

      Life gets more extreme
      as it goes on.

      I don't remember
      these temperatures
      going up and down
      so much

      Yet every bone aches with questions.

'Your mania for sentences
has dried up your heart.'

9.

Remember who you are speaking to——

       ——the strains of the Nutcracker heard
       from a radio station on the same frequency
       with the countdown
       for the first Los Alamos test——

       This turbulent ear hears turbulent news
       We will not bow to an obscene law

               I will piss on the elegant
and join you in your undersized armies.
I know you will lose.
We all do.
But you have your excuses

            Atlas of Ancient Dreads

Atlas of Ancient Youth
Atlas of Ancient Lust
You have your excuses

You need someone to lead you to ruin,
but I'm not the one. See the neighbours.

No one could name all their griefs.

       Train wheels going shut up, shut up, shut up

67

10.

The horse sinks knee deep
in silk
in America and the muck
the bruised flesh of the meadows
where politicians do not walk
stamping their feet like trains.

This is unsupportable.

I made these voices.

The arrangement is all.

It grew and grew until it was bigger than I was
and it made me think that I was bigger than I was.

The lie is elaborate and exact.

The cold miser sits chittering
in the old kitchen.

What good is a witness
who will not tell his tale?

& now I must wash and go.

I love you.

How long does it take you to decide
what to dream about? Do you think
carefully beforehand of women
you never enjoyed and who
would never agree to enjoy you?

Do you desire to dream of the deaths
of those you love so your sorrow
will be splendid among your friends?

Do you carefully build in your mind
your own car crash the police will announce
in tones that know your loss so well?

Do you rehearse your best tragedies,
distilling them into your dreams
night after night before your sleep,
your hair growing grey in your bed,
your pleasant tears huge on your head?

Or do you dream of a real loss,
the bent caverns of the dark sea,
the glass trees rough, shining at night,
no other animal in sight?

... and as soon as he was alone in the room (except for me) he sliced the baby up; in such amazingly thin, delicate slices. They folded and undulated like sheets of camera film too long soaked in water as he piled piece after piece of them over his bent forearm. Some of them were too slippery and they slid off his arm to fall on the floor and be trampled there. When he held them up to the light they were almost transparent, we could almost, not quite, see the world through them. What strange things they did to our view: how they distorted and disarranged and enriched everything, like some new paintings I have seen.

But I am not trying to be allegorical; when I say that we saw the world through a baby's flesh, I am not being allegorical. I would not want you to think that because of this strange modifier, panes of glass from a child's pain, that we saw new, wonderful things our eyes were not accustomed to, not that. Perhaps I should not have said *the world.* We only looked around the room and at each other; once, briefly, we looked out through the window at the grass and the trees, using the sheet of almost clear flesh we had in our hands at the moment, not any specially selected one. It did not really change things, nor did we look for changes, but there was something additional. We only used it as you would use a piece of dark glass or a black negative to observe an eclipse of the sun. But that sounds allegorical too. As if I were tying to make a point; I am not. It is only a manner of speaking. I am only trying to say that we looked at things through the flesh of a child to amuse ourselves, as it were, not to assume the vision, the viewpoint, not to assume the attitude and position of a child; only to amuse ourselves. We did not want to see the world as it really was, the room as it really was, ourselves as we really were, or to strip away the semblances, discover a master secret, the truth. None of that.

I told you that the sheets of flesh were nearly transparent. The blood was gone from them, yes. But they were not wholly transparent. I did not quite tell the truth. Apertures of the veins and arteries, sections of lungs and intestines, circles of bones – further up, the soft pink-grey discs of shell-encased brain, tiny – they all showed, they forestalled monotony, they were all beautiful. I have never quite seen paintings like them, though I hope to one day. Perhaps, sometime, I shall make such a thing, piling and unpiling arabesques. He did a fine, lovely job.

And it was easier than you think, much easier. At first he thought that certainly the bones would give him trouble. So did I. But all in all it was only a matter of assembling the proper machinery; in some cases, I may as well tell you, even of inventing and building it, though vaguely similar things have been known before. He is a clever man that way. So neatly, so cleanly, so thinly and perfectly to slice a baby up, that was nothing to him. To us it seems a great deal of work to do such a thing properly, but he enjoys it. So would I, so would you, if we had his skill in making and operating machines, the most delicate, precise instruments imaginable; so would we all if we shared his delight in conceiving of, in inventing these marvellous techniques. This is not the only one he has made. Think of the ingenuity involved! We do not possess it, but him, he's a master of such things. Or a past master perhaps I should say, since he has died now, alas. As we all will die. It seemed a special shame that he should be removed from us.

I cannot speak more of it. He is not dead to me. He is still alive and I shall probably speak of him, if only out of sentiment, as if he really were alive. His work lives on. That is a trite thing to say, that is what everyone says, but I am sure of it.

Babies' bones are soft. That's reasonable. So soft. At first he had thought that the bones would give him trouble and he was troubled about it. It seemed a sensible worry. But as things happened they, the bones, gave him no difficulty at all. Or very little. Because they were so soft. Certainly he should have thought of that. I suppose it is always best to be prepared for the worst, though, never to take chances. I can agree with that.

What he finally devised did the job wonderfully, butchers would have loved it; of course the idea of fat smiling butchers, men with the raw entrails of sheep and cows draped about their shoulders, vendors of dead animals to eat, men with blood and feces and wipings of their own snot mixed on their aprons, using a device like this, a wonderful device, is too horrible to contemplate.

It was almost too powerful; almost, not quite. Only a few pieces were spoiled. Since he had forgotten to consider how soft babies' bones really are; since it was such a young child.

Very soft, very soft. Softer than, softer than what? Softer, I suppose, than swan's down? It is the same colour, I know; it is white, the swans are white as bones are white. But how soft is it? That is what we really want to know. I have seen swans myself, I have seen swans float, glide, skate on a pond or on a lake, a lagoon, skate like modelled figures of white wax sliding across the surface of a mirror. I have seen those swans; surely there must have been wires under the water, about their legs, to guide them. They moved with such precision, with such serenity, never making a mistake in their inevitable purposeless paths. But how soft is their down? I cannot answer, I don't know. But it is said to be soft, they tell me it is soft. I myself have never felt it.

Softer than what? Softer than a woman's shoulder? But some of them are angular. Softer than a fat woman's shoulder? Some of them have tough crusty pimples, mysterious and disturbing lumps. Were the bones, then, soft as a woman's breast, thin or fat? But some of them have cancer or hard repulsive nipples, they get hard when they are cold. I cannot find an image, an adequate image, to tell you how soft the baby's bones were. Of course, I have tried only one really, and half of another. But I can feel that there is nothing that will work, nothing worthy enough to describe that softness fittingly. You will have to take my word for it.

I forgot to tell you how when he first took the baby into the room he angled its chin into a coathanger and slung it from the top edge of the door. That part of it didn't interest him at all; it was merely part of the necessary preparation and anything would do. Always, no matter what you attempt, it seems that there are so many details to be looked after if things are to be right. But still, he did it with a certain flair. Another person, myself perhaps, I admit it, or even you, would have rudely noosed a rope, some rough-fibred hemp cord, whatever was at hand, about its neck and would have hung it from one of those parallel bars in the clothes closet. That would have been a foolish thing to do, I almost laugh when I think of the alternatives now, considering the merits of the various solutions. Of course, it's easy to be wise after the event. But better to be wise after the event than never to be wise at all, neither before nor after. That's what I say. A rope, you see, would have bruised the neck badly, it would have left a great red ugly burn about the neck; the wire of the coathanger made only the most pleasing of thin scarlet lines, a delicate contrast.

He slit the long deep vein in the sole of its foot and bled it into a basin. Perhaps it was an artery, not a vein, he slit. I don't know. I am sure it was in the sole of the foot, the right foot. Or along the side of the foot, of the instep. He used one of those old-fashioned straight razors you seldom see anymore. They may still be used in barber shops, but I don't go into them very often. Not at all. I shave every morning and in the early evening with an electric razor, a remarkable instrument really, but not a very interesting one. My hair is cut at home, too. That's why I don't know if barbers still use those old-fashioned straight razors. I believe they do. And perhaps a few old dying men here and there use them. With their wire beards, slack skin, their trembly hands and rheumy eyes, I wonder that they dare. I suppose there's a knack to it one acquires. But that was the sort of razor he used. And very efficient it was, too. I don't know where he got it.

It cried some when the razor went in first. That's reasonable; babies cry at surprises. But we did not expect that after it had been hanging there, a good hour on the door for people to admire. How fine it looked. But it cried all the same, that is one of the things one must put up with. With which one must put up. And it wailed and it wailed. Not very loudly, thank god. What would the landlord have thought? People would have said, There's a child on the second floor, I can hear it crying.

No, it didn't cry very loudly; only a thin choked reed of a sound that could not be heard very far, that disturbed no one. It reminded me of something or other, I don't know.

The blood running down the door.

After cutting the vein he had taped ankle and toe of the child in such a fashion, in such a position, that the blood ran right down the door, not spraying or spurting out at us. With what a deft movement he did it, how dexterously he did these things, all things manual and machine-like and not only them. I wish I were like that; so do you.

I keep thinking of him in the present tense, by mistake, and it is an effort to change, as if he were still alive; I keep forgetting that he is not. I told you I would do that, I always do.

But not for very long. The blood didn't run down the door for very long. After all, how much does a baby weigh, one so young as that? Not more than fifteen pounds, I'd say. Maybe sixteen. It's hard to judge. But it would weigh about fifteen or sixteen pounds or certainly not more than twenty; and how much blood could it have in it? Not very much. It would be unreasonable to expect very much blood from a child of that size and that age.

Children's blood is lovely. Not that it looks any different from the blood of a youth or an adult, of course not. Or even the blood of an ape, of a pig, a cow. Even the blood of fish and lizards, of birds. But it is lovely, simply because, as you look at it, you do not imagine all the passions, the cunning, the secret urges and lusts, the perversions, even drugs or alcohol or nicotine swimming in it, diseases polluting it. This is subjective, I know that, but you do not imagine, whether it is present or not, ugliness in the blood of very young children. You see them pure and delightful and somehow you are pleased and proud.

It cried a bit when the razor first went in. I told you that. But I was wondering if *cried* was really the right word to use; I want everything to be right. No doubt you do too. That is a human trait, to want everything to be right, almost a failing sometimes, but usually good. Perhaps cried was not quite the proper, the completely accurate word to use. I want you to understand. It gave a long thin wail like the sound you would expect an adult,

not a child, to make as it bled to death. A very knowing
sound. Or as they say you may hear the hungry wolves
howl on a winter's night in the north while they circle in
their precarious, tortuous routes, devouring what rabbits,
soft rabbits and other small things, small favours, may
fall to them in their pathways; as the hungry and
dangerous wolves howl, but far off, very far off. If the
child had not been before my eyes I would have thought
it was some starving wolf away across the snow,
separated from me by a forest or two. Or another might
have thought it the sound of some lost fantastic primitive
man drifting far out at sea in a little boat, shaken, pushed
and pulled, and swaying in the waves of unfamiliar
waters, the currents of the sea, loosing and losing a
desperate prayer to his dying gods; you might have
imagined that it was him, heard on an alien shore by
ignorant and frightened tribesmen of another nation, to
hear that insolent child cry. It was like that and I cannot
recall now what it was that it reminded me of; of these
things, surely; yes, of these things. But they are only
made-up fancies, inventions, conceits to explain that
sound to you. They are not what I wanted to remember.
They, the hungry circling wolves, the lost and crying
man, they are not what evades me.

Then, as the baby bled, it seemed to grow very sleepy
and its body stretched out long and white and limp
against the dark brown door. And it looked fine there, it
looked exactly right. Long, long is not the word for it; it
was stretched out unbelievably, hanging there with its
muscles all relaxed, the bones seeming to melt, to turn to
fluid, dissolve.

Not all of them seemed that way, of course. The rib
cage in particular stands out in my memory as in fact it
stood out from the body, jutting out from the flesh, its
skin pulled tight over it. How good it all looked, with the
head angled far back and to one side, the eyes half-closed,

the lower lip sagging fatly but the top one tugged up over
the perfect pink gums, with the exquisite line of the
throat, the smoothness of the chest; and then, suddenly,
that wonderful protruding ridge of ribs to break the spell,
break the monotony, and the rest of the body hanging
without resistance, jelly-like, seeming to depend from it,
how good, how good.

Its body was very white. Alabaster, plaster. Like those
swans we were speaking of, or like snow in mid-winter
far out in the country, away from smokestacks and
kitchens, diesel engines, factories, mines; like snow then,
when you catch it momentarily and one flake at a time
with a gloved hand before it slips erratically onto the
ground and is crushed underfoot there, the snow through
which the wolves roam, white as the perfect paper,
unspoiled by human words. And that white against the
brown-stained door compared with the splash of blood in
the enamelled basin on the floor below it, what
dissonances these colours made, and what new harmonies
I discovered in their relationship.

It is when you know where a thing comes from that it
is most valuable to you. You would not have believed
that anything could be so white. I would not have
believed it, not even I. Startling, those three colours –
the dark brown, the pure white, the violent liquid red –
like the perfect colours of flowers, waiting to console you
for whatever you cannot remember.

The perfect colours of flowers. The perfect colours of
flowers are waiting to console you if you will only seek
them out, seek them out and never hesitate to
appropriate them and take them home.

I'd like to live a slower life.
The weather gets in my words
and I want them dry. Line after line
writes itself on my face, not a grace
of age but wrinkled humour. I laugh
more than I should or more
than anyone should. This is good.

But guess again. Everyone leans, each
on each other. This is a life
without an image. But only
because nothing does much more
than just resemble. Do the shamans
do what they say they do, dancing?
This is epistemology.

This is guesswork, this is love,
this is giving up gorgeousness to please you,
you beautiful dead to be. God bless
the weather and the words. Any words. Any weather.
And where or whom. I'd never taken count before.
I wish I had. And then
I did. And here
the weather wrote again.